This World Book Day 2022 book is
a gift from your local bookseller,
Ben Bailey Smith and Bloomsbury.
#ShareAStory

WORLD BOOK DAY

THE LAST WORD

BEN BAILEY SMITH

BLOOMSBURY
CHILDREN'S BOOKS
LONDON   OXFORD   NEW YORK   NEW DELHI   SYDNEY

BLOOMSBURY CHILDREN'S BOOKS
Bloomsbury Publishing Plc
50 Bedford Square, London WC1B 3DP, UK
29 Earlsfort Terrace, Dublin 2, Ireland

BLOOMSBURY, BLOOMSBURY CHILDREN'S BOOKS and the
Diana logo are trademarks of Bloomsbury Publishing Plc

First published in Great Britain in 2022 by Bloomsbury Publishing Plc

A catalogue record for this book is available from the British Library

ISBN: PB: 978-1-5266-4655-2

2 4 6 8 10 9 7 5 3 1

Typeset by RefineCatch Limited, Bungay, Suffolk

Printed and bound in Great Britain by CPI Group (UK) Ltd, Croydon CR0 4YY

To find out more about our authors and books visit www.bloomsbury.com
and sign up for our newsletters

For Harvey

CHAPTER 1
Gotcha

People say I've got a big mouth for a little guy.

Some people say I'm a know-it-all, a joker, a clown, a troublemaker. Other people say I'm cheeky, sneaky, sarky, snarky …

Who are these people? I hear you ask.

Well, basically everyone. At least everyone in my school at Wainbridge Academy, everyone in my area of Queen's Crescent in Camden, North London, and definitely everyone in my house.

That must be sad for you, I hear you add sympathetically.

Ha, I reply to whoever you are, *on the contrary, these 'people' are absolutely correct.*

And I love it.

You see, my name is Carmichael Taylor – Car for short – and what I lack in good first names I make up for in Last Words.

I always get the last word. Always. Don't believe me? Try me. Go on. Say something.

I'll wait.

Go on, off you go.

You can write it in here if you prefer:

That all you got? Fair enough.

What I'm saying is, for as long as I can remember I've refused to leave any situation without saying my piece, making a comment, hitting back and having that sweetest of desserts – the very last word. Like once when this tough kid in my year, Tosun Kendall, threatened to 'batter' me and I said I'd prefer breadcrumbs. His confusion bought me time to do a runner.

Or when my best friend Alex Kember and I accidentally set off a school fire extinguisher – it really was an accident, by the way. Alex wanted to know how they worked and I investigated a little too closely. Our Head of Year, Mr French, was not impressed. He dropped the classic 'And if Alex told you to jump off a bridge, would you do that too?'.

I paused for a second.

'If it was a bungee situation, I have to say I'd consider it, yes.'

I should stress here, I'm really not a bad kid. At least, I don't think I am. I'm thirteen years old, I'm the size of R2-D2, I've got hair like candyfloss and a freckly face that looks a bit like a dot-to-dot puzzle, but you'd better bring your A-game if you think you're going to outwit Car Taylor.

There's not a teacher on earth who's managed it yet, so if you want to feel sorry for someone, you can pray for those guys.

This tale is about one teacher in particular who found himself in what some of those people who talk about me might call 'a horrific Car accident'.

CHAPTER 2
Supply and Demand

There are all sorts of teachers. Irritable ones like Mr French, firm but fair ones like our Head Teacher, Mrs Craig, the odd cool one like my English teacher, Miss Miller, anxious ones like my Form Tutor, Miss Choudhary ... and then there are *the temps*. The substitutes. The infamous, unpredictable ...

SUPPLY TEACHERS.

Now, these guys are a breed of their own.

They look like teachers. They've got the teachy face, sure. They've got that teachy smell down to a tee. They wear teachy clothes, have all the teachy knowledge and even the teachy lines: *'If what you're talking about is so funny, why don't you come up here and share it with the class?'* (Quick tip to any teachy types reading this: NEVER make that offer to me. My public speaking game is kind of my forte.)

But what they don't have, the one thing they sincerely lack that they desperately need, is good old-fashioned day-to-day *knowledge*. And at Wainbridge, we revelled in using it to our advantage.

They don't know the layout of the school. They're unaware of certain procedures and timings, traditions and in-jokes. They don't know anyone's names ... Alex and I never failed to take advantage of *those* moments.

Now listen, I'm not saying it's right. We never want these guys to suffer, I guess we all just instinctively feel we can muck around more if our regular teacher isn't there. There's an old-timey saying. '*When the cat's away, the mice will play.*' That means this stuff's been around since the old-timey times. You can't only blame *us*, I mean it's practically tradition.

Anyway.

Early in the spring term (this was months before I shocked the world with something I said *live* on television, but that's another story – *wink emoji*), we found ourselves in just one of those moments.

'You. Over there. Yes, you, with the frizzy red hair.'

Our latest supply pointed at me and I pointed at my own chest.

'Me?'

'Yes. What's your name?'

'Julio Frankenfurter, sir.'

'Right … Julio. *Julio?* OK. Yes – can you please stop talking to … who's the young man next to you?'

'Sir, she's a girl! Just cos she's got short hair … That's actually very offensive.'

'Oh! Uh … Yes, of course. Sorry, I'm …'

'Don't worry, sir,' Alex chipped in, 'I'm Anita.' She pointed over to another girl, Natalie. 'But there's two of us. That's Anita Harrison, I'm Anita Pritchard, so you just say Anita H or P. Depending who you need.'

Natalie nodded and smiled in confirmation.

When the sniggers settled, this week's world-weary supply teacher, Mr Phillips, shifted uncomfortably on the spot and continued with his Science lesson on the elements. He was one of those men who could be twenty-five or forty-five. It was impossible to call because despite a full head of hair and unblemished, pale skin, he was also a little hunched over, wore glasses like my grandad's and had trousers with hard creases down the middle of each leg – trousers that no one under the age of forty should even know where to buy, let alone own.

He also had a stop-start way of talking that meant he never sounded sure of himself – he left way too many gaps between words that invited constant heckling. And we were pushing it today.

'OK. So. Let's … Let's look at how elements react to each other. Now we're – we're gonna do this in a *fun* way. So no – no more whiteboard for the minute. We'll do a little – a little role play.'

A collective groan.

I'm not sure who the first teacher was who thought *role play* was a 'fun' way of doing anything, but somehow one of the worst ideas in educational history had endured right on into the twenty-first century.

'Don't worry, it'll be – it'll be fun. So! I need three volunteers … Er … what's your name, sorry?'

'Mehmet. But you can call me Mo. You can call him Mo as well. And him.' Mehmet pointed out Mohamed and Tyler. To be fair, we did call all of them

7

Mo, what with Mo being short for Mohamed, Mehmet being Mohamed in Turkish, and Tyler being the footballer Mo Salah's biggest fan. This confused Mr Phillips even more, but he went with it. Mehmet jumped up and Mr Phillips stuck a sticker on his shoulder.

'OK, you're Carbon.'

'Wait, is that explosive though?'

'It can be!'

'Sick! Man's gonna blow!'

'Well ... er ...' Mr Phillips looked around the room for another willing participant. There clearly wasn't one.

'Want another Mo?' Mehmet offered.

'Sure.'

'Come, man.' Mehmet motioned to a reluctant Tyler. Tyler sighed and got up. Mr Phillips pinned a different-coloured sticker on him.

'Oxygen.'

'Ah what?' Tyler screwed his face up in disgust. 'Oxygen? That's one of the baitest ones, bruv. Everyone knows that one!'

'As they should,' offered Mr Phillips. 'They'd struggle to live without you!'

Tyler rolled his eyes.

'Now … One – one more. I need …' Mr Phillips scoured the room, then smiled as his brain landed on a name he thought he remembered and he declared joyfully, 'Anita P!'

The class held back snorts. I piped up, right on cue.

'The gents is down the hall, last door on the left.'

Laughter filled the room and Mr Phillips finally caught on to the gag. We watched his face turn a deep shade of crimson and bumped victorious fists.

'OK, yes, very – that's very funny, now please …'

Mohamed threw his hand up.

'Sir! Sir!'

Mr Phillips looked flustered.

'Yes, er … Mo?'

'Now I need a pee. Can I go to the toilet?'

'Yes, yes … OK …'

Mohamed stayed seated, gritted his teeth, tensed his face for a few seconds then relaxed, letting out a big sigh.

'Thanks, sir. Carry on.'

Another big laugh from the room. We were becoming a pack of hyenas, circling an injured antelope – in bad trousers. I started to wonder whether Mr Phillips's main area of expertise was Science or Gullibility. Bless him, he soldiered on.

'OK, you – Mo, *Mo One*, you place your hand on Mo – *Mo Two's* shoulder. What have they become? Anyone?'

I threw my hand up.

'Moses?'

Mr Phillips ignored that one and wrote 'x2' on Tyler's sticker.

'Anyone? No? Carbon ... Anybody? Carbon? Carbon ... *Carbon Dioxide* ... OK. Now, uh ... I'm guessing it's not your name, but *Anita*, you put your hand on and – excuse me!'

Tosun Kendall was talking loudly on his phone.

'Could you put that away please!'

Tosun looked up, pulled the phone away from his ear and held it to his chest ...

'I'm on a call, bruv.'

... Then carried on talking.

Mr Phillips's head and shoulders dropped. When he lifted them again I noticed his eyes widen, in what looked distinctly like fear, to something above and behind our collectively unruly bodies. I turned to follow his nervous gaze.

Through the glass panel in the classroom door stood Mr French, arms folded, glaring at Mr Phillips with one of his signature Mr French glares.

I'd seen it used a hundred times before on a hundred kids. OK, maybe a hundred times on eighty kids – twenty times were just me.

I knew that glare. It was sign language for three words:

1. My.
2. Office.
3. *Now.*

I'd just never seen it used on a teacher.

CHAPTER 3
Pandemonium

Pandemonium is one of my favourite words.

It's sort of grown to mean general chaos these days but it actually comes from a really crusty old poem we studied in English, written in the crusty old seventeenth century by a guy called John Milton, who was pretty cool considering he was probably crusty and old too. I mean, he just made that word up like a boss. He made up loads of words that we still use now, like *terrific* and *enjoyable* and even *unoriginal*, which would have been original when he came up with it, which is terrific and enjoyable.

Not unoriginally, the Pandemonium in Milton's poem was the name of a palace built in the middle of Hell and, judging by Mr Phillips's face in that moment, he'd just stumbled into the grand ballroom.

Mr French continued to observe the lesson through the window. He had a face of thunder but made no move to enter. Interesting. I nudged Alex and motioned to the door with my head. She raised her eyebrows at me and made a little 'o' with her mouth.

'OK, let's – let's … How about this? Who's musical?'

Mr Phillips had clearly reached rock bottom. He bent down behind the front desk and reappeared with – *oh God* – an acoustic guitar. As general chatter and laughter began to mix with bemusement, he pulled the strap over his shoulder and called over the noise.

'Anyone with a bit – a bit of rhythm?'

This was my time. The stars had aligned in a perfect combination: a raucous class, a supply teacher, and a boy whose mouth moved quicker than his brain. If there's one thing you should know about Car Taylor (other than a bad habit of referring to himself in the third person, soz), it's that he never misses an opportunity to perform for his peers.

I thrust my hand up.

'Ooh, ooh, me, sir, me!'

'Julio! Come on down!'

I danced to the front of the classroom, bowing and waving as the class cheered and jeered in equal parts.

'OK. Now, you – you just tap out a beat on the desk here. Can you do that?'

'Come on, sir, my dad was the drummer in a German flamenco band!' I pointed to myself and raised my eyebrows, reminding him: '*Frankenfurter?*'

'Oh wow, that's – that's …'

'Unusual,' I said as I tapped out a basic beat with my right palm and left fist.

'Nice … Little faster … Perfect.'

He started strumming.

'Now, I'm going to sing a song by a man named Tom Lehrer called *The Elements*. We're going to squeeze the name of every single element of the periodic table into two minutes. Ready?'

'Lemme give you a little intro, sir,' I offered.

'Er – right. OK … Here we – here we go!'

I kept tapping and started a basic rhyme.

> *'Hey, Mr Phillips …*
> *Hope that you're sure*

> *Cos it don't look too good*
> *With Mr French at the door!'*

Almost as one, the class turned to spot our Head of Year eyeing proceedings with a huge dollop of suspicion. Mr Phillips tried to cut me off.

'Uh, right. OK, here we go!'

But I was in full swing …

> *'I said hey, Mr Phillips*
> *Got stuff to pack?*
> *Cos you're gonna need it …*
> *When you get the sack!'*

The class went into full-blown mania – shouts, whoops, '*Nahs*' and an '*Oh my days, he went there!*' rang around the room.

Mr French burst in.

'Can we have a little order in here, please!'

The din continued.

'Hey! *Quiet! NOW!*' Mr French roared.

We shut up.

'Now, 8H, if you don't mind, can we finish the last

five minutes of the lesson at this level?' said Mr French with a forced calm. 'There are seven other classes on this floor, trying to concentrate.'

A quiet pause.

I stood awkwardly by Mr Phillips. His body language was like mine: like a kid who's about to face the music. He turned to me.

'Sit back down please, Julio.'

Mr French and I caught each other's eyes as I shuffled back to my seat. A frown crossed his face, and he gave me a look that clearly said, 'Julio?'

'Thank you,' said Mr French to the room, 'and thank you in advance for your participation in a full class detention, in your tutor room today at three thirty.'

A huge groan echoed around the lab, immediately interrupted by Mr French.

'It's your own fault. You've left me no choice!'

His roaming stare landed on Mr Phillips and he gave one of those classic Mr French smiles that wasn't really a smile.

'Mr Phillips,' he said simply, with a nod. Then he left.

Mr Phillips slowly lifted the guitar off his shoulders.

I'm pretty sure he did something approaching a gulp.

CHAPTER 4
Go Time

Detention meant Bubblehub was off.

Alex and I had planned to go to a juice bar in Notting Hill called Bubblehub that sold huge cups of ice-cold fruit cocktail 'bubble teas' with exploding jelly balls at the bottom.

'It's the stuff of a madman's dreams!' Alex had yelled. I'd never had one before and wasn't even sure if exploding jelly balls were things I wanted to digest, but it did sound like I should try it at least once.

No chance now.

A forty-five-minute detention meant that I wouldn't get back to Camden in time for dinner. Even if I could, Mum and Dad would have already been pinged a message about the detention and wouldn't let me go anyway.

My mum is pretty strict with stuff like that – she's a nurse and she's all about schedules and rotas and responsibility and decision-making and respecting her house or getting out, getting yourself a job and learning the value of things for once because she's just about at the end of her tether. Dad would shrug and nod a 'What she said' nod because his really strong, firm, individual opinion is whatever Mum's opinion is.

So there Class 8H sat.

3.47 p.m.

Seventeen agonising minutes in, Miss Choudhary was sat at her desk, marking. The rest of us were silently catching up on homework. Alex nudged me and nodded to the window, which looked out across the playground to the School Office reception. As my eyes followed hers, they briefly paused on her homework. She had drawn a crude self-portrait – an excited-looking cartoon-Alex sat in what looked like an oversized Coke can. Underneath, it said 'TIME MACHINE'. I didn't even begin to question why this full-page sketch might take centre stage in her exercise book for Spanish.

She nudged me again.

Mr French, the Head Teacher Mrs Craig, and Mr Phillips were stood outside reception. We couldn't hear the conversation, but the body language spoke volumes. Craig and French looked like a pair of disappointed parents and Mr Phillips looked like a four-year-old who'd just bitten a fellow nursery kid.

We watched as he sloped off towards the gate, guitar over his shoulder, cardboard box full of science in his arms, head slumped. Mrs Craig raised her eyebrows in a facial shrug and Mr French shook his head like a vet might before he tells you your hamster isn't gonna make it.

Alex and I exchanged a look that said, 'Ooh, that's *gotta* hurt.'

Like most pupils, in school terms past we'd given more than one supply teacher a war story or two to take to their next placement. We'd been the stuff of nightmares, I'm sure. But ... as far as I knew, this was the first time anyone had actually lost their job.

I felt a flush of heat in my cheeks, then a pang of panic that I quickly pushed down. *Maybe he was only ever gonna be here until the end of the day anyway,* I figured. *He's probably walking straight into his next job, right?*

I felt myself mirroring Alex's slightly pained expression, then shook it off with a shrug.

'Not our fault he couldn't hack it,' I whispered, adding a little carefree chuckle for good measure.

'Yeah,' Alex whispered back, attempting a small chuckle of her own, but I sensed she was struggling to add the *carefree* element. 'I guess.'

CHAPTER 5
Chicken City Limits

'I'm not saying I've invented it yet, I'm saying *who knows?*'

Alex coloured in some buttons on her time machine whilst simultaneously popping Rainbow Drops into her mouth as we trundled along on the 274 bus into Camden Town, post detention.

'*I* know.'

'No you don't. No one does. No one knows what the future holds. I might invent it somewhere down the line.'

I reached into her bag of puffed-up, sugar-coated, multicoloured rice and stole a fistful before she could squeeze the packet shut.

'Hey!'

'Al. Think about it. Let's say, OK, *yes*. Alexandra Kember invented a time machine in 2047. Her life's work finally realised.'

'Nobel Prize?'

'All the prizes. You wouldn't be sat here right now, would you?'

'Huh?'

'I know you. The first thing you woulda done is travel back to, like, 2016, bet all your money on Leicester winning the Premier League, be a millionaire by the end of primary school, and you'd be on your own island by now.'

'Mm. That is true. But maybe I'm trying not to mess with the space-time continuum.'

I pressed the bell as we approached our stop and we stood up.

'I don't buy that,' I said. 'Messing with stuff is like your default position.'

'My default? How can you say that's my default? No way is that my default … What's a default?'

'Like, your go-to thing. The first choice every time.'

Al kept pressing the button, making a rhythm of

the '*dings*'. The driver's exasperated voice called over the tannoy.

'CAN YOU LEAVE THE BELL ALONE, PLEASE!'

I raised my eyebrows at Alex, making a 'point proven' face.

'Oh,' she conceded.

'Yeah, "*Oh*",' I said with a smile as we hopped off the bus.

As we walked down the High Street we heard a shout from behind us.

'Ey! Charlie and Lola!'

We turned.

My older brother Malky, hanging out the door of Chicken City (clearly a cut above Chicken Town, Chicken Village and Chicken Cottage – a whole city!). He had a box of wings in one hand and was flanked by his best mates, TJ and Dane, all three of whom delighted in teasing me at any opportunity. Malky was like the inverted version of me: tall, athletic, non-freckled dark skin, and hair that I would describe as Normal Human Hair as opposed to Red Pigeon Nest. He called over, grinning.

'You off to the soft-play centre?'

I shrugged.

'We tried but there was already a group booking under your name.'

My only satisfaction in genetic inheritance over Malky was that I got the brains. TJ and Dane laughed at the burn. Malky screwed his face up.

'Oi! Come here.'

'Why?'

'Cos I said so.'

'We're going home.'

'What? You scared?'

'I'm not the one residing in *Chicken* City.'

'Come here, man.'

I sighed, nudged Alex and we headed over. Malky polished off a wing and dumped it on top of a stack of bones in his greasy box.

'Dane's sister said you got a teacher fired today.'

I shifted uncomfortably from foot to foot.

'What? No, everyone was … doing stuff.'

I looked to Alex as if she could confirm this. She nodded uncertainly. Malky narrowed his eyes.

'Playing with fire there, bro!'

'Yeah, well, don't worry about me.'

'When have I ever done that?'

'Touché.'

'Two-what?'

'Forget it, eat your grease.'

'You trying to be funny?'

I smiled up at him, my brave face fully on.

'I never try.'

CHAPTER 6
OK ...

D inner was curried chicken with rice and peas, for which the smell of Malky's chicken had very much whetted my appetite. I love my appetite getting *whet*.

To whet your appetite might sound like you're actually dampening it, but in fact 'whetting' comes from *whetstones* – a lump of rock that old-timey English folk used to sharpen their knives on – so when you smell a tasty smell or your stomach rumbles with hunger, you're basically just sharpening your desire to eat. Yes, I love dictionaries. Point is, my appetite was clearly sharper than Malky's as he was already full of Chicken City chicken. Shame.

'Not hungry, Malcolm?' Mum eyed his plate as he shuffled food around it.

'Just balancing the diet, y'know. It's race season.'

Malky was a sprinter for the Hampstead and Highgate Harriers, and he was so good it tended to mask a lot of his underachieving in other places, as well as his white lies and constant belittling of me. To my parents he was *The Boy Who Could Do No Wrong*. To me he was *The Boy Who Could Not Leave Me Alone*.

'Gotta watch what you put in that well-oiled machine,' I said pointedly, glaring at him.

'That's right.' He glared back.

'Cross-country was my bag when I was your age,' offered Dad. Mum, Malky and I exchanged a quick, knowing glance, ready for another anecdote we'd all heard a hundred times before. My dad Stuart is freakishly tall with pale skin and bright red hair – the mastermind behind my fiery frizz. I smirked.

'But you cheated, didn't you, Dad?'

'What?'

'Cos with those legs you could *cross country* in one step.'

'Very funny.'

'Thank you.'

Malky rolled his eyes, but Mum chuckled. I liked making Mum laugh. Jocelyn Taylor is small in stature, but massive in seriousness.

'So,' Mum said, changing tack, 'what was the detention for today?'

Well, that didn't last long.

I gave the tiniest, shortest flinch before regaining my composure.

'Didn't it say in the notification?'

Dad pulled out his phone.

'General disobedience, lesson disruption,' he said between mouthfuls.

'No phones at the table please, Stuart,' I said. Mum frowned at me.

'What did you do, Car?'

'It was a whole class detention! It wasn't just me!'

'But what did *you* do?'

'Nothing!'

Mum lowered her head and raised her eyebrows, shooting me her death stare. 'Really.'

I wobbled.

'I mean … It was … This supply guy lost control.

The whole class was mucking about. It's not like I was the instigator.'

Malky snorted. I shot him a glare.

'But you were involved.'

'I was just, y'know – *there*. Like everyone else.'

Mum still hadn't blinked. She carried on staring at me but addressed Malky.

'Something to add, Malcolm?'

'Nope!' Malcolm held both palms up, enjoying watching me squirm.

'OK,' she said knowingly. 'I mean, you wouldn't want to risk your big day out at the end of the month, would you?'

'What? No! Course not.'

Dad had been given three tickets for an Arsenal match at the Emirates Stadium as a gift for an engineering job he'd worked on there and – to my delight – had offered to take me and Alex along to our first ever live football match.

'Well, OK,' Mum repeated flatly.

'OK?' I offered hopefully.

She nodded and sat back, apparently relaxed.

'Yup, *OK*. It's always *OK* when you tell me the

truth. And it will continue to be OK when *you're* OK with knuckling down and *focusing*. Year Nine is no joke. You'll start your GCSE courses the year after … Things will get pretty serious pretty quick, Car, so as long as you're *OK* with all that then yes –' she smiled with a laid-back warmth that was somehow disturbing – 'we're OK.'

I shifted uncomfortably in my seat and looked over to Dad for support.

'Sounds OK to me!'

Course it does.

I glanced up at the football tickets, shimmering away like shiny treasures under a magnet on the fridge door.

'OK then,' I offered, and switched focus down to my plate, avoiding further eye contact.

OK.

CHAPTER 7

Heaven Help Us

'What about her?'

I shook my head.

'Nah.'

'Hmm … *Her?*' Alex pointed at a second woman, middle-aged and blonde in dark glasses, weaving across the road through stationary traffic as we sat on the bridge wall above the canal at Camden Lock.

'No way.'

'Why not?'

'She looks nothing like you!'

'Yeah, but if I was coming back from the future to find myself I'd disguise myself so as not to scare myself when I met myself. Obviously.'

'Obviously.'

A ping. I pulled out my phone. Alex nodded over at it.

'How long you got?'

'She's nearly done. Should probably head over now.'

It was Saturday, and Alex and I had been loafing around Camden, people-watching and discussing all manner of lofty subjects – not just time travel but also going to see Arsenal play, how ears grow rapidly when you get old, what your last ever pudding for your last ever meal would be and who would win in a fight between Ed Sheeran and Ned Flanders. Mum meanwhile was doing the big shop at Sainsbury's on Camden Road with no car, so we'd been roped into meeting her outside to help carry the bags home.

As we headed towards the tube, Alex suddenly stopped in her tracks, pulling me to a halt too.

'Oh my DAYS!'

'What? Wait – don't tell me. Your future self, here to warn you not to—'

She nudged me and shook her head, cutting me off.

'Crazier than that, bro, check it.'

She jutted her chin towards the station where, with an acoustic guitar and an upturned hat on the ground at his feet, stood a dishevelled Mr Phillips.

If you don't know what *dishevelled* means, wait until tomorrow morning and the second you get up – but before you go to the bathroom or do anything else – have a look at yourself in the mirror. You'll have the meaning right there, literally staring you in the face. I'm not sure if when you're super slick and smart and tidy you could be described as 'shevelled' … but I'd like to think so. It would have given Mr Phillips something to aspire to. As it was though, he was giving off distinct scarecrow vibes and both Alex and I looked on, from a safe distance on the opposite side of the main road, as he cleared his throat and introduced a song.

Alex pulled out her phone and zoomed in as best she could.

'This – so this … This next one,' Mr Phillips began in his trademark fashion, 'this is original. It could be available on all digital platforms but it's … I mean at the moment it's … well, it's not, but …' The small crowd around him laughed at his awkwardness, but warmly – enjoying the distinct lack of boasting from this strange performer. 'Anyway, yeah. Um, OK … This is – this is called *Heaven*.'

He strummed away and delivered a first verse with a quick-fire melodic flow, kind of like a farmer rapping.

'I'm camping out
Under the stars
In a deep dark wood
Where you can't hear the cars
Pitched up in a bog and my pillow is a log
And the last passer-by was a green tree frog
And the gas ran out
So I ate beans cold
From the can
I'm a man, thirty-three years old
BUT!

'This is Heaven compared to yesterday
Cos yesterday owned me
Now I'm blessed to say I'm free, oh yeah ...

'This is Heaven compared to yesterday
I've got algae in my pants
And been bitten by red ants, oh but ...'

34

He sang the chorus with certainty, and though his body language was still shy, I was quietly impressed by how he could switch from nervous speech to weaving these intricate rhyme patterns in song. And his singing voice was small but sweet and oddly powerful. And he was funny! And he was thirty-three. I'd learned a lot of new information in a very short space of time.

Alex looked back at me with a similar face to the one I imagined I had.

'Wait, he's actually kinda good!'

'Right?' I nodded back. I checked my phone. 'Come on, my mum's at the checkout.'

As we turned on to Camden Road, Alex watched back her recording. She laughed.

'"*Algae in my pants*"! He's funny.' She stopped the video on her phone and looked to me. 'But it's also kinda sad.'

I shrugged this off.

'He seemed happy enough.'

'Listen to the lyrics, man! He's, like, putting a brave face on a life of tragedy!'

'Yeah, but it's not necessarily about him. Could be a character.'

'What, about a guy who's standing on a pavement dressed like a castaway singing for change, perhaps?'

I scoffed. 'Come on! He was *entertaining*. It's an act.'

'Well,' said Alex, 'he looked real to me.'

'So, what? What are you saying?'

Alex shrugged.

'I dunno. Nothing. Just … I dunno.'

Inside the sprawling and busy supermarket, Mum leaned against a window, surrounded by a selection of bags collected over various years before. Alex and I hurried over.

'You took your time.'

'Sorry.'

'Here.'

We stood like Christmas trees as Mum loaded us up and the three of us waddled out, laden with goods. Alex swapped one heavy bag from her left to her right hand and puffed out her cheeks.

'You having a party, Mrs Taylor?'

'What?'

'Uh …'

'It's the big shop.' Mum shrugged.

'Clue's in the name, I guess,' I said.

'Yeah,' said Alex, wincing slightly. To be fair, she'd got a lot of the baked beans.

Turning back on to the High Street, Alex and I exchanged an awkward glance as we realised Mum was taking us right past Mr Phillips. We let Mum move ahead of us and we instinctively skulked by with our heads down.

Just as we thought we had avoided any potential unpleasantness, we heard a call through the bodies of passing pedestrians.

'Julio?'

Alex and I exchanged a worried glance.

'Julio! H-hey!'

We went to catch up with Mum but before I knew it, there was a hand on my shoulder.

'I *thought* that was you.'

Mum turned and a question formed on her face. I thought fast. I called out to her, pointing down to the busking spot.

'Hey, Ma, we're just gonna have a look at these CDs quickly!'

'We'll catch you up!' Alex threw in.

Mum rolled her eyes.

Mr Phillips seemed calm and pleasant. But seeing any teacher out of school is always, *always* weird – let alone one you made unemployed less than a week ago.

'Sir?' I offered.

'Yes! Yes, it's me. Mr – Mr Phillips. Well, just – just Sam now, but … Yeah. Ooh, one sec.'

He spun round to grab his hat, and Alex and I looked at each other, both of us wondering whether to make a run for it. But before any silent pact could be finalised, he was back, all smiles.

'Ten, eleven … Nearly twelve pounds! And I've only been here three hours.'

Alex and I nodded politely.

'Every penny counts now.'

'Yeah?'

'Well, the teaching agency has let – let me go since … I'm not sure Mr French gave me a good, um … Anyway. Are you guys having a good day?'

'Car!'

My mum called out.

'We, uh – we have to go,' I said. Alex held up a bag.

'Fish fingers. You can't refreeze 'em,' she said. But she had a look of genuine concern on her face. 'Sorry – do you … Do you want … Do you need a fish finger? Or … anything?'

Mr Phillips – or just Sam – laughed and shook his head politely.

'If *Anita P*, I'll let you know.'

He turned away, pouring the change from his hat into his hand and plunging it into his pocket. We watched him shuffle back to his spot. As we turned to leave we both nearly jumped out of our skins – Mum was nose to nose with us. She daggered us with her eyes wide, then narrowed them in suspicion.

'Who was that man?'

I shrugged.

'Some busker.'

Mum nodded.

'Didn't get a CD then?'

Alex looked over to where Mr Phillips was tuning up with no CDs in sight.

'It's all online now,' she offered.

Mum nodded again.

'Right.'

She paused for a second.

'Why'd he call you *Julio*?'

CHAPTER 8
The Trouble with Mums

The trouble with mums is they know everything and everyone. At least, mine does.

If you walk down the High Street with Jocelyn Taylor you have to stop and chat with every other person you pass and they ruffle your hair and ask you what year you're in at school and say things like, 'Haven't you grown?' and, 'The last time I saw you, you were only up to my knee!' and then they expect some kind of a response that is more than a shrug. All of which means what should be a ten-minute walk becomes an hour-long marathon.

Then there was the gossip. Actually, it wasn't so much gossip that Mum was into – it was *facts*.

Mum loved new information, preferably from the

horse's mouth. Weird phrase that, isn't it? *The horse's mouth*. Horses don't even talk. Even if they could, I don't think the first thing they'd tell you would be the latest gossip. I reckon it'd be, 'CAN YOU GET THIS LAZY HUMAN OFF MY BACK! LIKE, NOW, PLEASE! YES I WILL HAVE ANOTHER APPLE.'

Anyway.

Over dinner that evening, I found myself unsettled by the way Mum kept talking casually to Dad and Malky about 'Car and this busker' as if she were prodding me for information without asking me directly. You see, my mum didn't necessarily need the horse's mouth to tell her what she wanted to know. She had back-up horse-mouths all over Camden, a network of horsey spies she could call on to fill her in on anything she might have missed.

I went to my room early, feeling distinctly uneasy. You know when there's something you need to do but you can't quite work out what it is? Like those dreams where you're meant to be somewhere important but you can't quite get there and you don't even know where *there* is and you have a shirt and hat on your top half but just underpants on the bottom? OK, maybe that's a little too specific, but you know what I mean.

In these situations, there was only ever one thing to do: contact a *higher power*. A *spiritual guide*, a *wise mentor*, a *guru* of sorts.

I reached for my mobile.

The call was answered before the first ring even sounded.

'Good evening and welcome to Alexandra Kember Enterprises, where *your* problem is *our* problem. Alexandra Kember speaking, how can I help?'

'Wait, how did you know I have a problem?'

'Wild guess. Look at your face.'

'You can't see my face.'

'I mean in general.'

'Idiot.'

'So whassup?'

'I dunno ... I think—'

'Wait a minute. How much cheese do you think is too much cheese to eat before bedtime?'

'What? Um ... How much have you had?'

'Hard to say. It's squeezy cheese. I dunno how many slices a tube and a half is equivalent to.'

'That's too much.'

'I think I'm hallucinating.'

'Put the tube down.'

'It's like brain freeze without the freeze. It's brain *cheese*.'

'I'll just chat to you tomorrow ...'

'Whoa, whoa, whoa, no – wait a sec ...' A loud belch. 'OK, I'm good. Go.'

'I think ... I think I feel ... *Ugh*. I hate to say this about a teacher but ... Al, I think I feel *guilty* about Mr Phillips.'

'*Ohmygosh* same!'

'Really?'

'Why do you think I'm lying in bed drinking cheese? I'm literally smoothing over the cracks in my conscience with preserved dairy liquid. I'm in a bad place, bro.'

'But what can we do?'

'I mean, is there anything we *can* do?'

'I've just got this horrible feeling. Not just about Mr Phillips living in a cardboard box somewhere because of us, but also that, if my mum finds out, we can kiss those Arsenal tickets goodbye!'

'Oh man, the game! No *way* we're not going!

There's literally nothing more important than that! I mean, the cardboard box thing as well …' She paused. I heard a small slurp down the line and winced. 'Hmm. Tricky. Tell ya what, lemme go wash this cheese down with some squirty cream and clear my head. I'll sleep on it. I'm better in the mornings.'

A second wince from me.

'Cream? Having a real dairy party over there. Why not add a nice room-temperature glass of goat milk while you're at it?'

'Eww. Gross. Later.'

'Later.'

CHAPTER 9
Blueprint

'I've got it!'

Sat at the bus stop on Monday morning, I looked up from my phone to see Alex bounding towards me. I beamed back at her.

'Tell me!'

She flopped down next to me, exhaled giddily and spread her arms out, raising her hands high and wide as if she were unfurling a giant banner. She spoke slowly and dramatically.

'*We get Mr Phillips his job back.*'

'Right, yeah, I mean that's what I was thinking last night. How?'

'I hadn't got that far.'

I slumped in disappointment.

'Hey, I can't come up with everything!' Alex said cheerfully.

The bus came and we hopped on.

'Let's think about this strategically,' I said. 'Who would we need to convince?'

'Mr French?'

'Deffo.'

'Mrs Craig …'

'Absolutely.'

'Maybe him too.'

'Who, Mr Phillips?'

'Yeah. Like, maybe he's happier doing the whole wandering-minstrel thing. The whole rope-for-a-belt vibe.'

'I don't think so. But you're right that we should start with him. Now how the heck would we get a Head and a Head of Year to listen to us and rehire the guy?'

'Well,' Alex thought aloud, 'what makes him different from all the other supply teachers we've had?'

'He's the worst?'

'And the most tragic.' She nodded apologetically. 'I mean, he came to school with an actual guitar.'

My eyes lit up.

'Al, you're a genius!'

'Don't say that until we bump into my future self.'

'The *guitar*. That's our way in!'

I spent the rest of the day dreaming. *Daydreaming* – the most regular word on my school reports after 'talkative'. I was formulating a grand idea, playing it out in my mind – I was gonna help a guy, shake this guilt, make amends *and* have fun doing it. It wasn't just a win-win. With those four benefits, it was a win-win win-win. And actually, if I also got to go to Arsenal AND they won, it'd be a win-win win-win win-win. That's just maths.

Alex and I raced each other all the way to Camden Town station, a plot firmly built and shared between us. We followed the sound of live music through a small crowd outside the station, only to find a band of Peruvian pan-pipe players, all dressed in colourful ponchos. It hadn't occurred to us that Mr Phillips might only be there on Saturdays.

We waited for the musicians to take a break, then approached the one who seemed like the leader, as he offered his CDs around a rapidly dispersing audience.

'Excuse me,' I said.

'Five pounds,' he responded.

'Uh, I'll … get one next time. Listen, have you seen a guy who plays here sometimes? Acoustic guitar, dresses like a supply teacher?'

'Three pounds,' he offered.

'No, I—'

Alex tapped my shoulder, stopping the awkwardness in mid-flow. She pulled out her phone and showed the guy her video of Mr Phillips. She spoke slowly in stilted English for his benefit.

'Hell-o, sir. Have. You. Seen. This. Guy?'

The band leader squinted at the screen, then replied in perfect English, much to Alex's embarrassment.

'Oh yeah, that's Sammy – he's hilarious. He plays here Saturday lunchtimes, sometimes Wednesday evenings, I think.'

It was only Monday. If Mum was already in Sherlock Holmes mode, even Wednesday could be too late.

'I don't suppose you know where he lives?'

He shrugged.

'I dunno. He looks kinda homeless. Tell him Hector says hi.'

'Thanks, man,' I said.

'You got it. You want a CD?'

'We don't have any cash. We'll ... we'll stream it.'

'OK, be good.'

At dinner that evening, I was so desperate to steer the conversation away from school that I actually engaged my brother in conversation, asking him one too many questions about an upcoming track event he was competing in.

'What are you, my biggest fan now?' he asked.

'I'm being supportive!'

'Well, stop, it's weird.'

I appealed to Mum.

'You try and do a little good in this world and that's the thanks you get.'

'They say *no good deed goes unpunished*,' offered Dad.

'Who says?'

'*They* do.'

Malky screwed his face up.

'What does that mean?'

'It means,' began Mum, 'that whenever you try to

help someone, it backfires on you. Perhaps the person you helped is ungrateful or maybe your kindness is taken for a weakness. But I don't believe it's true.'

'Neither do I,' Dad agreed.

'Didn't you just say it though?' Malky asked.

'I said, *they* say.'

'Oh yeah.' I smiled. '*Those* guys.'

'Point is,' continued Mum, 'it's a negative outlook on life. You shouldn't stop doing good things just because you're afraid something bad might come of it. You should do good things because you feel *compelled* to do good things.' She paused and looked at me. 'Naturally.'

She knows, I thought. *Or maybe she doesn't. But maybe she does. The woman is unreadable.*

'You know your mother is doing a good thing up at Wainbridge on Friday,' Dad threw in. I hid a mild panic at the idea of my mum being at the scene of my crime anytime soon.

'Oh yeah?'

Dad rubbed Mum's back proudly.

'Yup. She's gonna be one of the speakers at the Careers Fair for the Sixth-Formers. Inspire a new generation of nurses.'

'We'll see,' Mum said humbly.

'That's awesome, Ma,' I said, nodding.

I looked at my watch.

Is it Wednesday night yet?

CHAPTER 10
Julio Comes Clean

O n the pretence of a cinema trip, Alex and I headed straight back to the busking spot after school that Wednesday. There was no one performing, but we were going nowhere. We bought three-pound meal deals from a nearby Tesco and sat on a bench to wait. Alex munched nervously.

'What if he doesn't show?'

'He'll be here,' I said, more trying to convince myself than anything.

I elbowed Alex and she coughed on a sushi roll.

'Oi!'

'Look.' I pointed. 'Speak of the devil.'

Mr Phillips shuffled into the busking spot, laid down his hat and pulled his guitar over his shoulder.

With no introduction and no audience to speak of, he began singing.

'He was the colour of caramel
We used to walk parallel
Lamp posts? He'd have a smell
And empty his bladder well
Sometimes he'd eat an old tissue he'd find
And none of my personal issues he'd mind
Short fluffy beard, big glittery eyes
He barked real loud at delivery guys
Then came the day that I couldn't afford him
But at the rescue home they'd feed and board him ...

'Derek! Oh, Derek
There'll never be another Derek
I said it, I meant it
I'll miss you, old friend

'Derek! Oh, Derek ...'

As the doleful chorus continued, I slowly turned to Alex in horror. Her eyes had glistened over.

'Al, please tell me this is another joke song.'

'I think I need to go home and tell the goldfish I love her,' said Alex, through a mouthful of Monster Munch.

'Oh man, this is too much. Come on.'

I hopped off the wall and Alex followed me to where a small crowd had formed in front of Mr Phillips, who was now wrapping up his last chorus.

'Derek! Oh, Derek
When I see you again
Know I saved up, never gave up
To get you back in the end.'

He gave a sad little strum and patted his guitar. A smattering of applause echoed around the onlookers.

'That – that was called "Derek". I'm Sam the – Sam the Guitar Man. I hope you're – hope you're all having a good day.'

I pulled Alex to the front.

'Mr Phillips!'

He beamed when he saw us. Not sure why. We ruined his life!

'Julio!'

'Sir, can we talk to you for a minute?'

'Sure! What's up?'

I looked around at the small audience.

'Maybe somewhere quieter?'

We went to Alex's favourite cafe where they make really greasy bacon rolls and do hot chocolates for a pound. She ordered three cups and the drinks came moments after we'd taken our seats at one of those little tables with the plastic chairs attached. Mr Phillips took a big slurp and smiled.

'So. What can I do for you?'

Alex and I looked at each other.

'Sir ...'

'*Sam.*'

'Sam,' I repeated awkwardly. 'We wanted ... we wanted to say sorry.'

'Sorry?'

'Yeah,' we both said in unison.

'For what?'

Another glance between me and Alex. Why do adults always make apologies so hard? They have to make you crawl through all the gory details.

'Well, for … *y'know*.'

Mr Phillips looked genuinely confused.

'Er, no …'

'For … getting you fired and stuff.'

'What? Julio, you didn't get me fired. *I* got me fired. Think about it. Do you get up and muck about like that with every teacher?'

'He kinda does,' said Alex.

'But not like that,' I countered.

'Right. And why not?'

I shrugged.

'You feel they're stronger because that's the air they have! I just – I just don't have that air.'

'You've got loads of air, sir!'

Nice one, Alex.

'I wasn't good enough.' His turn to shrug. 'That's – that's it.'

'That's it? But sir, don't you want to, like, try again?'

'Sure, but who'd have me? I need a – a reference to get back on the teaching agency. I'm hardly gonna – gonna get that from Mr French. I don't – I don't think he likes me.'

'That doesn't mean anything. Mr French doesn't like anyone.'

Mr Phillips let out a little chuckle and looked down at his cup.

'Well. I should get back to my spot. Guys … I – I appreciate the – the concern, and the – the apology. Honestly. And I'd give anything to teach again, but I think that ship has sailed.'

Alex and I exchanged a panicked look. This wasn't going well. He stood up and we both instinctively jumped up with him.

'Sir!'

'*Sam.*'

'Sorry, yeah. Listen. We think you're a good teacher. And the music-with-science thing. It's actually kinda cool – right, Al?'

She nodded vigorously.

'Innovative.'

I fixed my eyes on Mr Phillips.

'What if there was a way to go back?'

'Julio …' He sighed.

I mirrored his sigh.

'OK, my name's not Julio. I'm not half German,

half Spanish, and my surname isn't Frankenfurter.'

'I'd forgotten the surname. It *is* quite implausible, now that I—'

'My name is Carmichael Taylor and ... well, I'm kind of a big deal.'

Alex screwed up her face.

'People listen to me.'

Mr Phillips laughed.

'Well, hello, Carmichael. Although that – that also sounds like a joke name ...'

Alex snorted. I glared at her. Mr Phillips continued.

'... And goodbye, Carmichael. Good – good luck.'

He headed towards the door. Alex elbowed me and I shouted after him.

'Wait! What if I told you we had a way of getting you your job back by the end of the week?'

He stopped in his tracks and turned back.

'I'd say you were wizards!'

I smiled to Alex and she called over to Mr Phillips with glee.

'Well, *Avada Kedavra*! Come with us!'

Mr Phillips furrowed his brow.

'Isn't that a death curse?'

Alex widened her eyes. 'Is it? I thought it was like *Abracadabra*?'

I shook my head at Alex as we led the way out. 'You really should read those books.'

CHAPTER 11
Come On, Man

'Carmichael, that's crazy,' Mr Phillips said, shaking his head as we wandered back towards the busking spot.

'Why?'

'Because … because it just is! I mean, even if I could write the perfect song and you got everyone to hear it, even if Mr French loved it, how does that guarantee my job back?'

'Leave that to me,' I said with a confidence that I hoped hid the fact that I had no idea. For now, the plan was simple: 3.30 this Friday afternoon, Mr Phillips would give a performance so brilliant, so loved by every child and staff member, that Mr French and Mrs Craig would *have* to have him back. And all would be right in the world again.

Mr Phillips returned to his busking spot and placed his hat back on the ground. He looked down at us.

'I dunno, guys. I don't think – I don't think it's a good idea. Sorry.'

He turned to various semi-interested passers-by.

'O-OK, folks. S-sorry for the interruptions. This next song is about …'

Suddenly Alex turned and shouted, 'What about Derek? Don't you want to see him again?'

Mr Phillips turned to us, a pained expression on his face, then continued.

'This – this song is about toenails. We've – we've all got 'em!'

He cleared his throat and began,

'Who knows what this is
Misters and misses
Some might be short or as long as a witch's …'

'Let's go,' I muttered to Alex.

'No,' she countered. 'We wait. I'm telling you – Derek got to him.'

We returned to the bench opposite and sat through a collection of funny and sad songs – they were always that mix. Bitter-sweet, hilariously tragic or melancholy with a laugh-out-loud twist. For a guy as unsure of himself as Mr Phillips, he could write a strong lyric.

We watched him count up his money, then made a beeline for him. He sighed as he saw us.

'Guys, seriously—'

I cut him off.

'Here's the deal. You go home, relax, count your millions. Tomorrow we write the best song you've ever had. Friday, you perform it at Wainbridge and get your job back. Saturday, you go pick up Derek. Sunday, we celebrate.'

He shook his head and gave a rueful chuckle.

'You make it sound so simple.'

'You got a better plan?'

'Carmichael …'

'Car.'

'Car. How do you expect me to come up with something that good in one night?'

'With help,' I said, pulling out a piece of paper

from my back pocket. I handed it to him. 'Meet us tomorrow at four p.m. for a musical masterclass.'

He took the scrap of paper, looked at the address I'd written, then looked back at us curiously. With no further words, I beamed at him, confidently spun on my heels, nudged Alex and we marched off, job done. Alex whispered over to me as we walked.

'Reckon that worked?'

'I have absolutely no idea.'

CHAPTER 12

Uncle Godmother

The address I'd given Mr Phillips was my Uncle Landon's first-floor flat in Camden Town. Lan's my mum's younger brother and an actual professional musician, the best I know.

Also the only one I know.

Every Thursday, he and Alex had a backgammon match after school that I usually tagged along to, so he wasn't surprised to find us on his doorstep at ten to four. But he was slightly taken aback by the mass of information I was piling on to him in the ten minutes we had before a strange guitarist would arrive, desperately seeking his help.

Once he was up to speed, he smiled.

'I like it. It's the Cinderella story. And I'm

the Fairy Godmother, right?'

'Exactly.' I smiled. Uncle Lan was the best. As siblings go, he and my mum were so different. She was all fire and ice, and he was … warm, relaxing bathwater. That sounds weird now, but you get the picture.

'Which makes you two the Ugly Sisters.'

'Yeah, yeah.'

The intercom buzzed and Lan pressed the entry button. A small, uncertain knock tapped at the door and I was relieved to see Mr Phillips, guitar in hand, on the other side.

'Sam, right?' Lan beamed. 'Come, come!'

He waved him in and Mr Phillips glanced around in wonder at the array of instruments strewn about. Lan offered Mr Phillips a fist bump and Mr Phillips offered Lan a handshake. Nice and awkward.

'I'm Lan, Car's uncle. This is where the magic happens!'

'Uh – yeah. Car – Car told me he was a wizard. Of sorts.'

I smiled bashfully.

'I'll get the kettle on,' Alex offered. Lan nodded.

'Let's get to work.'

'You still there? It's nearly seven!'

'Yeah,' I replied into my phone. 'It's a marathon match this week. Alex is on fire!'

'Well, put her out and get my brother to make you some dinner, we're eating without you.'

'I will. Thanks, Mum.'

I hung up and turned to face the gang. Alex was tapping away on some bongos and Lan was showing Mr Phillips a new bassline he'd come up with. We'd been at it for three hours straight, functioning on cups of tea, Jammie Dodgers and Haribo. Mr Phillips looked flustered.

'No good?' asked Lan.

'No, no, it's – it's great,' Mr Phillips began, uncertainly. 'Musically, it's … You're really good and … I just … We still don't have a good lyric.'

'What are you talking about? The lyric is great! *The teacher, the preacher, the incredible creature* … Come on!'

'I dunno,' said Mr Phillips. 'I don't – I'm not …'

'What?' Lan looked at Mr Phillips with genuine concern. Mr Phillips took a deep breath.

66

'All my – all my songs. They – the point of them is they're self ... self-*deprecating*.'

'What's that mean?' Alex asked.

'They're built to punch me in the face, y'know? Like – I'm – I'm the butt of the joke. I poke fun at *myself*. But – but this ... It doesn't feel right. Me talking about being such a good teacher and ... y'know, *how great I am*. I mean, I'm not a *rapper*.'

Lan lit up.

'Wait. Of course! Sam, you're a visionary, my brother!'

'I – I am?'

'Car, get a pen and paper. We're gonna blow this thing sky high!'

CHAPTER 13
Gift of the Gab

F riday was nervy.

Not nervy enough to stop me falling asleep in Geography, but it had been a long night – I hadn't got home until after 9 p.m. and had then stayed up into the small hours playing the plan through my head, over and over. I awoke to the familiar sound of a detention being issued but that was the least of my worries right now.

I had work to do that lunchtime and I needed to conserve energy.

After I'd eaten, I made my way to Mrs Craig's office and tentatively knocked on the door.

'Come in!'

'Hi, miss.'

'Mr Taylor. Is there a problem?'

'Uh, no, miss. Actually the opposite.'

'Oh?'

'Yeah, uh, my mum, Jocelyn, is coming in after school …'

'Yes, we're very grateful.'

'Yeah, and, uh – she was wondering … She's quite nervous and she was wondering if you could meet her before she goes in. Give her a pep talk, kind of thing.'

'She's never struck me as the nervous type.'

I shrugged.

'First time for everything.'

'Hmm. OK. But I won't have long. I have a staff meeting.'

'Five minutes, miss. If that. *Three* minutes. Just at the gates.'

'Three minutes.'

'Yes, miss.'

'Fine. Anything else?'

'No, miss. Thanks, miss.'

'Off you go.'

But there *was* something else: a repeat performance of that exact conversation down the hall, at Mr French's office.

'I rather think your favours ran out at the end of Year Seven, Carmichael. Or have you forgotten the fire extinguisher? The escape of the gerbils? Mr Parker's trousers?'

Yup, old Frenchie was gonna be a harder nut to crack.

'No, sir, I've not forgotten ...'

'And as I recall, you definitely weren't sat quietly in a corner desperate to study during that disastrous Science class the other week, were you?'

I shifted uncomfortably on the spot.

'Well, that was ... That was mass hysteria, sir.'

'Mass hysteria.'

'Yeah. Anyway, sir, this isn't a favour for me. This is a favour for my mum. Someone who's doing a huge favour for the school, you have to say.'

'Hmm.' Mr French frowned.

'Mrs Craig said she'd say a few words. As manager of Careers Week I was hoping you could do the same, but it's fine. You're probably busier than she is, I guess. Thanks anyway.'

I turned away.

'Carmichael.'

I stopped and smiled with my back still turned. *Got him.*

'Three thirty at the gates?'

I spun round, my face a picture of humility.

'Yes, sir.'

'I'll see what I can do. Go on.'

I practically danced out of the room.

I met Alex by the football space.

'What's the latest?'

Al had been rounding up audience members from our tutor group, laying on the potential for entertainment as thickly as she could.

'I've got pretty much everyone.'

'Killer!'

'Live music and free Haribo.' She shrugged, waving one of ten big bags we'd bought as bribes. 'It's a winning combination.'

I puffed out my cheeks. Al furrowed her brow.

'You ready?'

'I think so,' I said, then nodded firmly. 'I *know* so.'

I hoped so.

CHAPTER 14

Live from Wainbridge Academy

We literally ran out of Art on the stroke of 3.20 and pegged it to the gates, playing sheepdogs as we moved, herding up everyone we could, plus any stragglers we met at the gates. Outside, Lan sat on a large speaker with a nervous-looking Mr Phillips shuffling on the spot next to him. Lan jumped up when he saw us.

'We good?'

I looked back at the growing number of kids that Alex was marshalling behind me.

'We're good.'

'Are you sure about this?' Mr Phillips asked.

'You just do your thing, Sam,' said Lan. 'Be yourself. What have you got to lose?'

'I dunno. What's after job and dog?'

'That's the spirit! Come on,' Lan said to Mr Phillips, then called out, 'Over here!' and two guys pulled a few wooden pallets from the back of a van. Lan helped stack them on the pavement, then placed his speaker on top, plugged in a mic and his bass guitar, and got one of his mates to plug the speaker into the cigarette lighter in the van. *This guy!* I looked on in wonder.

I clambered up on to the pallets, helping Mr Phillips up afterwards. Lan tapped the mic and handed it to me. I took a deep breath.

'Wainbridge, what you saying?!'

Alex whistled and hustled the crowd of around thirty-five kids as close to the makeshift stage as she could. They cheered – mostly at the novelty of the situation, I expect.

Over the heads in front of me, Mr French and Mrs Craig were approaching at pace from the playground, looking mightily concerned. At the same time, a cab pulled up to my right and my mum stepped out and paused, narrowing her eyes at the sight of not one but two family members stood precariously atop a pile

73

of wood making a scene outside an educational estab-lishment. At the back of the growing crowd I spotted Malky with TJ and Dane pushing to see what was going on, then signalling to some other Year 10 kids. A distinct buzz filled the air.

It was now or never.

'Ladies and gentlemen,' I said with a smile, hiding my nerves. 'I wanna introduce to you a face you might remember, and a voice you'll never forget! Make some noise for Mr Phillips, aka Sam the Guitar Man!'

Mr French, Mrs Craig and Mum all stood with jaws at similar depths as Lan plucked out a bassline and Mr Phillips started strumming. I held the mic under his chin as he did his thing.

> *When I was young*
> *I wasn't small*
> *I also wasn't very tall*
> *Not a fool but not the smartest*
> *Not the slowest, not the fastest*
> *Hard-working but not the hardest*
> *Creative, but not an artist*
> *Twelfth place in the spelling bee*

A. V. E. R. A. G. E.
Style never came with age
Favourite colour? Prob'ly beige
Yes I'm singing on a stage
But technically it's bits of crate
I guess what I'm trying to say
Is I'm not terrible or great
I'm just somewhere in between
And good is good enough for me!'

Then Lan leaned over to the mic and joined in with a harmony as they both belted out the chorus:

'So gather round and watch, watch, watch
My bubble won't pop, pop, pop
And I won't stop, stop, stop …
Till I've made it
All the way up …'

They paused, stopped playing for a split second, and we all looked to each other to deliver the last words:

'To the middle!'

A big laugh and cheer from the crowd and the music kicked back in joyfully. Alex and the Three Moes were pounding their palms against the pallets with glee. Then it was my turn.

'Wainbridge Academy,' Mr Phillips called out, 'please welcome your very own ... *Carmichael Taylor!*'

I pulled the microphone back and steadied myself as what was now the majority of Years 8, 9 and 10 whooped and hollered. I watched Lan, who counted me in, mouthing *'Four, three, two – go!'*

I cleared my throat and pointed at Mr Phillips:

'Don't listen to him
Just listen to me
Cos I got a few words for Mr P
He says he's average
And trying, bless him
But who brings guitars to a Science lesson?
We could've behaved
But none of us tried
Meanwhile this guy's one of a kind!
Dunno about you but instead of regret
I'd rather have a teacher that I'll never forget

76

He'll say he comes up short in every test
But when it comes to Supplies? This guy is the best
Not saying much when you think of the subs
That we've had in the past, still I'm bigging him up!
He's cool, got a big heart, big passion
Even if his trousers are a crime against fashion
So shout it out, and sing with me
When I say, "Bring back," you say, "Mr P!"'

Over the cheers, Lan, Alex, the three Moes and I called out:

'*Wainbridge! Bring back?*'

And pretty much every single kid in front of us yelled the response in unison.

'*Mr P!*'

'*Wainbridge! Bring back?*'

'*Mr P!*'

'*Wainbridge! Bring back?*'

'*Mr P!*'

'*All right, cool. That's it from me!*'

I dropped the microphone on to the makeshift stage and raised my arms like I'd just scored the greatest goal in history. Mr Phillips strummed a big finish, and the crowd went bananas.

'OK, show's over!'

Mr French started dispersing the crowd. Mrs Craig made a beeline for me, looking stern. Mum followed closely behind, arms folded, but she seemed curious rather than angry. *I'll take that, whatever it is,* I thought.

'A word, Carmichael.'

I hopped off the pallets with various kids patting me on the back. I felt sheepish in front of the Head. Mr Phillips sat on the edge of the stage, looking even more sheepish.

'Outrageous,' Mrs Craig said firmly, 'unauthorised and, frankly, presumptuous.'

I looked at my feet.

'That said, I don't technically have authority over you once you're past these gates, and as much as I do not approve of being hoodwinked, I appreciate your sentiment and the earnest support of a staff member. A former staff member ...'

She looked over my shoulder.

'Mr Phillips?'

He jumped up and hurried over.

78

'I shall have a word with the agency on Monday.'

We both beamed and Mrs Craig held up a warning finger.

'I'm not promising anything apart from that phone call. The rest will be up to you and your own professionalism.'

'Of – of course. Thank you, Mrs Craig.'

She turned to my mum.

'Mrs Taylor.'

'Hi.'

'Quite a son you have there.'

'Yes. Quite.'

'Good luck. I mean that.'

Mrs Craig headed back through the gates, followed by Mr French glaring at me, leaving both Mum and me to wonder if she meant the Careers Fair or the prospect of raising me, or both.

Mum looked at me steadily.

I looked at my feet.

'Sorry, Ma, I should've have told you from the start …'

'Oh, I knew from the start.'

I looked up.

'Huh?'

'From the second he called you Julio on that Saturday, I smelt a rat.'

'But how—'

'I have my sources, Carmichael,' she interrupted, 'and a mother's intuition. I'm not happy you lied to me, but you went ahead and tried to right a wrong. I'm actually proud. I mean, you really need to work on your flow, but … I'm still kind of proud.'

I baulked.

'What do you know about *flows*?!'

'I wasn't born in the Jurassic period, Car. Rap existed when I was thirteen too.'

Wow.

Not bad for a mum.

As Alex, the three Moes, Lan and Mr Phillips bowled over, we exchanged celebratory high fives and fist bumps.

'Smashed it!' Tyler exclaimed.

'Amazing, bro,' said Mehmet.

'Executed my plan to perfection,' said Alex.

'*Your* plan?' I laughed.

'When I get the time machine sorted, first thing

I'm gonna do is come back here and watch the show again.' She looked out over the dispersing crowd and scanned it with a furrowed brow. 'Wait, maybe I'm here already!'

Mr Phillips took my hand and shook it vigorously.

'Thank – thank you, Car. Seriously. I didn't – didn't realise I needed that as much as I did.'

'You're welcome, sir. Hope we see you back!'

'Me too. Oh hey, wanna see someone else come back?'

'Huh?'

'I'm picking up Derek tomorrow if you want to meet him?'

'Sure!'

And we did. It was two killer Saturdays in a row, actually. Alex and I went with Mr Phillips to a dog rescue charity in East London and met his border terrier, and it was kind of emotional seeing them reunited. I mean, I don't know how cool it is for a grown man's only apparent friends to be two thirteen-year-olds and a dog, but in that moment it felt cool to me.

What was even cooler was that Dad had a

deadline to meet the following weekend and had to stay home doing all sorts of boring paperwork, so he looked after Derek, and Mr Phillips took me and Alex to the Emirates Stadium to watch Arsenal, which was totally awesome even though Arsenal were rubbish and lost two nil.

Looking around the tens of thousands of miserable faces I couldn't help smiling to myself.

I thought back happily to performing up on those crates, following Mr Phillips with that epic rap.

You can always turn things around. I did.

And I still got the last word.

THE END

About the Author

Ben Bailey Smith began his career as a rapper known as Doc Brown before diversifying and moving into mainstream TV and film acting, stand-up comedy, screenwriting and children's books. He has a host of notable television performances under his belt, as well as creating the BAFTA Award-winning Children's BBC TV show *4 O'Clock Club*.

Have you read

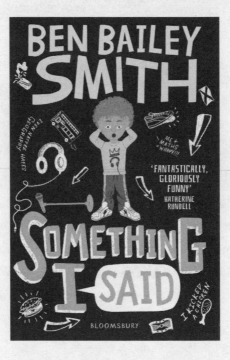

'Fantastically, gloriously funny'
Katherine Rundell, author of *The Explorer*

A blazingly funny, big-hearted story about family,
friendship and how far one boy will go to get a laugh

OUT NOW!

When Alfie sets an electrical creature loose,
it's going to be a perfect storm of trouble …

Read on for an exciting extract from this funny, heartfelt
adventure story …

1

Moth Man

17th July

I'm not sure how you're meant to start journals, but here goes: We moved to Folding Ford in April and now it's July, and maybe it's because we're new here, but to me it's completely obvious that this village is cracked. Today the weirdness got major, which is why I'm going to start writing it all down. If something happens to me, everyone will know the facts, because of this journal.

Here's what happened today:

Only little kids believe in giants, but that's exactly what pounded down the hill, right at me. I was standing on the bridge at the edge of the village. It was dusk and I should have been home already.

He closed in fast, crazy white hair flying out, long string

of a body, big coat swinging with every step, like a cloak. And, OK, so up close I could see he wasn't a giant, but he *was* a ginormously tall man with a creepy face from a nightmare ... and butterflies flapping around his shoulders.

The road was empty, the houses quiet and still.

Tried not to stare, but he was too tall, the butterflies were just too strange, and his snarly mouth and angry, darting eyes made him look ready to spring at anyone for any reason. I pretended something had got stuck in the front tyre of my bike, but my eyes were glued.

He scanned my face, a split-second glare that sent chills pulsing down my spine, chills that didn't stop, not even when he marched past me and away. And those weren't butterflies. They were brown, thick-bodied moths. And each one was tied to the man's wrists by a tiny thread.

He was taking them for a walk.

The giant with the moths is just the latest in a whole load of very strange things. Just in case anyone finds this notebook when I'm dead, here's a list of all the weird stuff that's happened since we moved here:

1. *A frozen puddle all by itself on a hot day in June. (Mum thought someone had emptied out their ice box on the pavement, but that was partly my fault. I shouldn't have prodded it before showing her.)*

2. *Thick frost on one branch of one tree near the primary school. Brilliant white, totally arctic and completely impressive (especially for June).*
3. *A whirlwind in one of Dad's beaten-up buckets, bubbling the water into demented spirals, and no wind anywhere else. (A salty smell came off it.)*
4. *A type of cloud I haven't seen in any other place. It's like a stack of pancakes with gaps in between.*
5. *My new best friend Sam's trainers iced up right in front of his eyes. He's been helping me look for clues ever since.*

All those weather freak-outs have *got* to be connected, so Sam and I are on high alert for clues about this weird overload. My new Moth Man discovery is completely different, but he's linked – I'm sure of it. Sam and I will figure it all out and maybe get famous from it, and then this journal will be the official record of how we solve the mystery of Folding Ford.

2

Fight! Fight!

<u>22nd July</u>

A massive day for the investigation! Discovered a HUGE amount of stunning new knowledge. Mum dragged us to a pointless jumble sale in the stupid village hall, and that's how it started, because guess what? The Moth Man was there.

As soon as he walked in, the entire room went quiet. Everyone turned to stare. The same mad hair streamed down his back. The same coat flapped behind like a giant bat had got loose. But no moths.

I grabbed my sister. 'Hey, Lily,' I whispered. 'Who *is* that?'

'How should I know? But whoa – he is so completely gigantic. Imagine how long his innards must be.'

'Remember the man with the moths I told you about?' I pointed at the Moth Man. '*Him!*'

Lily rolled her eyes. 'Give it a rest, Alfie.'

'For real. I swear.'

The hall was so quiet you could hear rain pouring off the roof.

I leaned closer to Lily. 'Look at their faces. Nobody likes him.'

'That lady does,' Lily said.

The Moth Man was rummaging through a stall full of electrical junk run by an old black lady – the only black person other than Dad that I've seen since we moved here – with silver beads threaded through her hair and a walking stick. He poked about impatiently, picking up an electrical extension cable without looking at her, even though she was talking nicely to him and smiling her head off.

The jumblers started to murmur again, softly, an up-and-down tune full of questions. Loads of eyes watched him hand money over, and he was every type of awkward a human can be. Kind of cross, but embarrassed, and also maybe in a massive sulk, like he hated the whole world. And he still gave me shivers.

'Ugh – looks like he's getting ready for something deadly. Someone so creepy shouldn't be buying that much cabling,' Lily said, like she was an expert.

'Look at his coat,' I said. 'Looks like it's made of skin.'

The Moth Man was on the move. This time, I had to

follow. He's the best clue I've seen since we moved here: a man who takes moths for a walk on a lead and turns a whole room silent. He *must* be something to do with the weirdness of this village.

'What are you doing?' Lily said, but I ignored her.

The Moth Man's coat still dripped. His hair looked like a dog's fur just before it shakes off the rain, and people made a big gap to let him pass.

I was brave. I got *sooo* close. Could have reached out and touched. The coat wasn't skin after all, but some oily fabric I've never seen before, and it smelt of horsey sawdust. He reminded me of a whopping, untrustworthy spider, and I got all jumpy again. I quite like spiders, but that feeling doesn't seem right for a human.

Mum blocked me. 'Where do you think you're going?'

'Just—'

'Oh no you don't. Mind your own business.' She gave me the stare of destruction.

The Moth Man was stomping off on heavy boots that would probably have liked to kick a few legs on the way out. Slipping away. Soon there was no sign of anyone towering and battishly cloaked.

'Can we just go, then? Home? This is for old people.'

'Nope. We're here to stay, and it won't kill you. We're still the new ones round here. We have to show our faces.'

'As if anyone's even noticed us—'

'Don't argue with me, Alfie Bradley. Stay where I can see you. Don't break anything – in fact, don't *touch* anything. And don't forget to say "please" and "thank you".'

Lily popped up behind her. 'Yeah, Alfie, zero touching. Got it?'

What was I supposed to do? I toured the hall, but there was nothing cool in the entire room, just stinky clothes piled on tables like junk mountains. Bo*ring* – until Lily came up to me, giggling behind her hand.

'There's a full-on shouty-crackers fight in the kitchen,' she said, signalling me to follow. It didn't look like a Lily wind-up, and Mum was bending over a stall.

'They're arguing about your giant,' Lily said. 'He rescues weird animals from abroad and they keep escaping and Mr Fuming says it's dangerous and Mrs Cranky says it isn't.'

'Who? *Who?*'

She took me to a tiny corridor between the main hall and the kitchen. The kitchen door wasn't completely closed, and through the gap we could see the old lady from the electrical-junk stall leaning against the counter. She was the one rowing, and she was doing it with an old man I hadn't seen before, and because the noise from the main hall was like a million murmuring penguins, we were the only ones listening.

This new old man was red in the face and bulgy in the neck, with bristly white side-hair sticking up round the edges of his bald head like a brush. Lily was right – they were having a fantastic blow-up, shouting over each other like we're not supposed to at school. All I understood was, *Don't ever invite him to a parish event again!* (The old man spat that.) And, *Don't you dare tell me who I can and can't invite!* (The old lady yelled this.) And then they stopped and glared at each other.

'You missed the best bits,' Lily said. 'She kept telling him to get knotted.' She put her earbuds back in and skipped away.

I got into perfect secret-listening position, like a detective: body hidden in a corner, head angled round. See without being seen.

The old man started up again. 'This village hasn't been the same since that miscreant came back.'

The lady rapped her fingers along the counter and gave him an impressively fatal scowly look.

'As head of the parish council, I have a duty to police his mess and botching.' His voice was croaky, and deep, like a walrus. 'We've had enough of his marauding animals – they're always escaping. That monstrous bird on the allotments last summer – the damage it did! Spiteful-looking creature. Vermin! Folding Ford is no place for zoo rejects.'

Then he aced it. 'All the children are afraid of him

and it's not the sort of thing we want in this village. Experimental animal breeding, warped hybrids – it's not right. Hellish goings-on at that house.'

The lady made a superb lip-puckered face at him and said, 'Ash House is an animal *sanctuary*, not a—'

'Don't play the innocent,' he snapped. 'We've both seen what's escaped from there. A stampede of giant mutant guinea pigs last spring! Ash House is a charnel house!'

The lady looked at the ceiling and groaned. Whatever a charnel house is, she doesn't like them.

Ash House. The last house in the village. I knew it straight away – we drove past when we were still exploring new places to live, just before we moved here. It's big, white, and stands on its own with huge fir trees in the garden. Those trees are the best ever. They sway in the wind, leaning together like they're whispering.

More shouting. More muddle. I couldn't see what was so bad about bringing things into the country from abroad and making wind traps and messing about with stuff and inventing junk – sounded cool to me – but the old man thought it was bad, bad, *baaad*.

'… you name it, he's dragged it back with him like a bagful of Beelzebub's beetles.' He stopped to snigger at his own cleverness, then went on even more spittingly than before. 'Greasy, poisonous things – all those spitting frogs.

And now he's tampering with the electricity supply! All those contraptions of his should be smashed and stopped. Every last one of them.'

'Don't be ridiculous!' the lady said. 'Nathaniel Clemm is harmless. You're the one who needs stopping.'

So the Moth Man was called Nathaniel Clemm.

'Harmless? Spinal cords lying around the place, and you call that harmless?'

Spinal cords!

'Well,' the lady said, 'vultures have to eat.'

'Vultures!'

'Just one vulture,' she said, drumming her fingers again. Her nails flashed silver, like Christmas decorations. 'And she didn't stay long – he was just sheltering her between zoos. He's a conservationist, not a butcher. You want to round up anyone who's not the same as you, don't you? You can't stand people who are different.'

With a ridiculous walrus-like '*Harrumph!*' the old man turned his back on the lady and stomped out of a side door. The lady looked like she might come my way, so I sneaked back into the main hall and blended in like a total spy. The investigation was going better than I could possibly have hoped, but what was the next step?

Suddenly it was obvious: I'd go and look at this spooky old charnel house myself.

Thought I'd got past Mum easy. She was trying to make Lily eat a cupcake, which is just about impossible because Lily hardly eats anything since she got bullied super badly when she moved up into Year Eight last year. (That's why we had to move here, to get Lily a brand-new life.) Anyway, Lily and Mum were in a cupcake standoff, but Mum must have clocked me, and just as I reached the door, she struck.

'Where do you think you're off to now?'

Never even knew she *could* creep up on people.

'Need fresh air,' I said. Then a brainwave happened. 'And can I meet up with Sam? I've done nearly an hour here.' Sam would freak when I told him about Nathaniel Clemm and Ash House. We could recce the place together.

She looked at me suspiciously.

'It'll give me more exercise …'

Her mouth stretched into a straight line with dimples at each end, which meant I'd won but she still disapproved. 'Go on then. But you're going nowhere without this.' She pulled out my blue padded monstrosity of a coat from nowhere that made any sense.

'Not that puffy thing! It's hardly even raining now.'

'No coat, no go. You *will* need it, and you *will* take it.'

I grabbed the evil thing and cleared out.

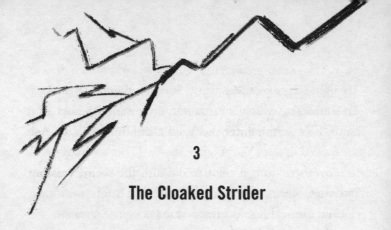

3

The Cloaked Strider

Persuading Sam to come with me was easy – at first. Went home for my bike, then texted, *Meet me at Eggshell Bench. Got intel!*

Sam: *What intel?*
Me: *Too long – tell you in person*

(That sounded professional. I'm getting good at this.)

Eggshell Bench sits at the top of stone steps on a steep grass banking, and you can hide there because it's always overgrown. It's one of our best places. The back of the bench curves over like a smooth plastic eggshell – like it got dropped on the way to a children's playground – and that's how it got its name.

By the time I'd biked there the stupid rain had stopped,

so never even needed my senseless puffer coat. I was tying the horrific thing to the saddle when Sam arrived. I thought he'd be excited, but even when I told him my whole entire intel, he wasn't up for going to Ash House.

'Can't see what it's got to do with the weird weather whatsoever.'

'But, Sam, this is our best clue yet. This might be the source of all Folding Ford's secrets,' I said majestically and watched him thinking. He's in the top set in all subjects at school, and sometimes you can hear his brain working. 'And it's a charnel house.'

'A *what*?'

'Yeah, sounds awful. Needs looking up.'

Sam got it done before I'd taken my next breath and said, 'It's a house full of bodies or bones, or *death*!'

'Whoa. See?'

'Still don't fancy it,' he said. He stared at his front bike wheel, scraping it with the toe of his trainer.

My belly felt like beetles were crawling in it and I went hot all over. 'Why not?'

'He's *well* scary. We call him the Cloaked Strider, because he walks round in that big long coat like a total randomer. Roan used to have nightmares about him.'

Roan is Sam's little brother. 'So the giant on Beggar's

Hill with all those moths – that was the Cloaked Strider?' I said. 'You never told me.'

'You didn't mention any cloak. You were all about a giant with moths on threads – which is impossible, actually. Moths shed scales if you even pretend to touch them.' Sam lives on a farm; he knows the most amazing stuff about any animal. 'If you tried to tie threads on moths, they'd slither away leaving you totally scaled up.'

'Which doesn't stop it from being true that day. I know what I saw.'

He shook his head at me, slowly. 'Anyway, he's *properly* weird. Dodge Cooper's brother says he comes out at night like a bat, and never sleeps. I'm not going near him.'

'But if we just do a little spy work from the road,' I said, rolling my bike down the steps and hoping he'd follow. 'It'll be fine. Come on – he won't even know.'

'There was no Cloaked Strider when my trainers iced up,' Sam said. 'The cold was just suddenly there and I stepped right into it. I'd have seen him.'

'That old guy made it sound like he does things from a distance. We might be able to see his long-range weather-warper machines through the hedge.'

Sam's face went very still and he scanned the village below us, like he was connecting things in his head. Like bits of curiosity were sprouting in his brain. I could almost hear them glooping together.

'We totally need to find out if that old guy's on to something.' I'd reached the road by now. 'Need to find out what a *miscreant* is. Sounds like something worth seeing – probably a deformed monkey, or something.'

'Nope. Not what it means. A miscreant is a kind of villain.'

'Only you would know that,' I said, but he pretended he hadn't heard and let a long sigh bubble out through pressed-together duck lips.

'A villain!' I said. 'Even better. Even more likely to be up to weather-warping business … especially if he's breeding dodgy animal mixtures. Weird goes with weird. Maybe he's planning to whip up a massive storm of mutant clouds that can push through doors and windows and suffocate everyone. Maybe he's lacing them with chemicals. And there are *spinal cords* lying around up there and everything!'

'Spinal cords? Where? How?'

I shrugged. 'Could be anywhere.'

Sam rolled his bike chain forward and back. It didn't need any fiddling, so I knew his brain was chewing through things. Then he bombed to the bottom step, did an excellent wheelie and skidded on to the road.

'Right,' he said. 'Are we going or not?'

If you enjoyed this World Book Day story, you might also like:

The Gifted, the Talented and Me by William Sutcliffe

Fifteen-year-old Sam is not a famous vlogger, he's never gone viral and he doesn't want to be the Next Big Thing. In fact, he's ordinary and proud of it. But all that is about to change …

A whip-smart and hilarious look at fitting in, falling out and staying true to your own averageness

Cardboard Cowboys by Brian Conaghan

When school gets too tough, Lenny always goes to his bench to think. One day as he's chucking his empty can into the canal he's stopped by Bruce. Bruce lives in a cardboard home tucked down by the banks, and he doesn't approve of kids messing up his front lawn …

A funny, life-affirming, unforgettable comic drama

The Valley of Lost Secrets by Lesley Parr

September 1939. When Jimmy is evacuated to a small village in Wales, it couldn't be more different from London. Green, quiet and full of strangers, he instantly feels out of place. But then he finds a skull hidden in a tree, and suddenly the valley is more frightening than the war.

A mesmerising mystery about bravery and brotherhood

WORLD BOOK DAY
3 MARCH 2022

YOU ARE A READER

Here at **WORLD BOOK DAY** we know that young people who read for pleasure do better in other areas of their lives and we want that for every young person in the UK and Ireland.

NOW YOU'VE READ THIS BOOK YOU COULD:
• Swap it • Read it again • Recommend it to a friend • Talk about it

WHERE WILL YOUR READING JOURNEY TAKE YOU NEXT?
We believe that there is a book for everyone. Why not challenge a friend, teacher, local bookseller or librarian by asking them to recommend you something?

THINGS TO THINK ABOUT WHEN ASKING FOR A RECOMMENDATION!
• I really liked… (*What should I read next?*)
• I like books that have… (*character types, plot types*)
• I am interested in…
• I would like to try… (*genre or non-fiction or poetry*)
…can you recommend a good place to start?

We believe **BOOKS AND READING ARE A GIFT**, and this book is our gift to **YOU**.

#WORLDBOOKDAY

WORLD
**BOOK
DAY**
3 MARCH 2022

WHERE CAN YOU FIND YOUR NEXT READ? YOU CAN...

1 TAKE A TRIP TO YOUR LOCAL BOOKSHOP

Booksellers like nothing more than the challenge of finding the perfect book for someone. Don't worry if what you want isn't on the shelf, most are happy to order specific things in.

Find your local bookshop:
booksaremybag.com

2 JOIN YOUR LOCAL LIBRARY

Libraries are a great way to take a risk on a book for free. Most library services have an online catalogue so you can browse at home and even order books to be delivered to your local branch.

You can also access magazines, ebooks and audiobooks online at home or on the go, with your library membership.

Find your local library:
gov.uk/local-library-services/

3 CHECK OUT THE WORLD BOOK DAY WEBSITE

There are so many ways to find your next favourite book. Talk to your friends and find out what they're loving, or even check out social media like Tiktok and Instagram to find the latest top recommendations. You can visit worldbookday.com where we have brilliant reads for you to discover and videos of some of our top authors to enjoy.